D1402717

For my beloved teachers, Rabbi Janet
Marder and Rabbi Yoshi Zweiback
CY

To LaMon, who knows all about cows
KH

Text copyright © 2022 by Caryn Yacowitz
Illustrations copyright © 2022 by Kevin Hawkes

All rights reserved. No part of this book may be reproduced, transmitted,
or stored in an information retrieval system in any form or by any means,
graphic, electronic, or mechanical, including photocopying, taping, and
recording, without prior written permission from the publisher.

First edition 2022

Library of Congress Catalog Card Number 2021953335
ISBN 978-1-5362-1654-7

APS 27 26 25 24 23 22
10 9 8 7 6 5 4 3 2 1

Printed in Humen, Dongguan, China

This book was typeset in Charcuterie Serif and Charcuterie Flared.
The illustrations were done in acrylic.

Candlewick Press
99 Dover Street
Somerville, Massachusetts 02144

www.candlewick.com

Shoshi's Shabbat

Caryn Yacowitz   illustrated by Kevin Hawkes

CANDLEWICK PRESS

Long ago, on a farm near Jerusalem, there lived a beautiful young ox named Shoshi.

For six days each week, Shoshi pulled the heavy plow through farmer Simon's fields, cutting deep furrows in the rocky soil.

On Shabbat, Simon rested.

So did Shoshi.

Every Shabbat, Simon's grandchildren played
hide-and-seek with the little ox.

They fed her sweet hay and
brought her cool water to drink.

As time passed, farmer Simon felt the weight
of his years.

"I am too old to guide the plow," he told his
family. "It's time for me to rest."

Simon sold Shoshi to his neighbor Yohanan, who had recently come to the hills near Jerusalem. Yohanan did not always understand the ways of his Jewish neighbors.

"Shoshi will help you plow and plant your fields before the winter rains arrive," explained Simon.

Simon's grandchildren hugged Shoshi.
"We will miss you," they whispered.

The next morning, Yohanan's children gathered around Shoshi. "Can we play with the little ox?" they begged.

"No, I have work to do," replied Yohanan as he yoked her to the plow. Together they tilled his fields.

Shoshi plowed for six days.
Yohanan was pleased.

On the seventh day, just as the doves stretched
their wings to soar over Jerusalem, Yohanan
placed the yoke on Shoshi.

She planted her four feet on the ground.
She bent her head low. She closed her eyes.

"We have fields to plow," Yohanan said firmly.

Shoshi did not move.

"Come!" Yohanan urged her.

Still, Shoshi did not move.

Yohanan stared at the little ox.

"Maybe you are sick," he muttered, removing the yoke. He led her to the shed.

"My fields will not get plowed today," he grumbled.
Instead, he began to repair an old harness.

Yohanan took no notice of the clear autumn sky
or the fresh breeze.

The next morning, the new day dawned pink and gold. Yohanan went to Shoshi. She was waiting for him.

"I guess you are feeling better," he said.

Together they plowed his fields, turning the soil
row by row. Yohanan was happy for six days.

But again, on the seventh day, Shoshi
would not budge.

"This will not do!" cried Yohanan,
pulling her from the shed.

He tried to place the yoke on her, but Shoshi tossed her head to the right. She tossed her head to the left. She stamped her feet.

"You are lazy, Shoshi!" Yohanan declared,
throwing the yoke to the ground.

Soon he felt a gentle breeze on his face. He heard the distant hum of bees among the grapevines and the sweet voices of his children singing silly songs to the little ox.

Early the following morning, when dark and dawn are blended so perfectly that the hour has no name, Yohanan awoke and went to Shoshi. There she stood, her ears up and her head stretched eagerly over the shed door.

Yohanan scratched his head. "I don't understand what's going on, Shoshi, but I'm glad you will plow today!"

They tilled his fields for six days. The earth was almost ready for planting. Soon Yohanan would sow barley and winter wheat. But on the seventh day, again, Shoshi would not budge.

"You are stubborn, Shoshi!" Yohanan cried. "Stubborn as an ox!"

Later that day, Yohanan was walking alone when he noticed a familiar figure in the distance. It was Simon.

Yohanan waved to Simon. Simon's prayer shawl billowed in the wind as he sailed after his prancing grandchildren.

The prayer shawl seemed to lift Simon up over the hills.

Shabbat, Yohanan thought. Today must be Shabbat, the day when Simon and the other Jewish farmers do not work.

Today is also the day when Shoshi will not work, Yohanan realized. She works for six days and then she refuses to budge.

He shook his head. Could it be? She is only an ignorant beast. And yet . . .

Yohanan ran to Shoshi. He stared at the little ox as she napped in the straw.

I am a clever man, he thought. *She is a simple ox. Yet I work seven days a week, with no day to rest, no day to give thanks. Perhaps Shoshi is the clever one.*

That afternoon, Yohanan's children gave Shoshi sweet hay to eat and cool water to drink. They played hide-and-seek with her among the fig trees.

Never again did Yohanan work on Shabbat. Nor did Shoshi, nor did any of Yohanan's other animals.

Instead, every Shabbat, Yohanan strolled with his family in the olive grove. He breathed the sweet air and listened to the chattering of birds and the humming of bees. He smiled at his children's silly songs.

Yohanan rested. He gave thanks.

So did Shoshi.

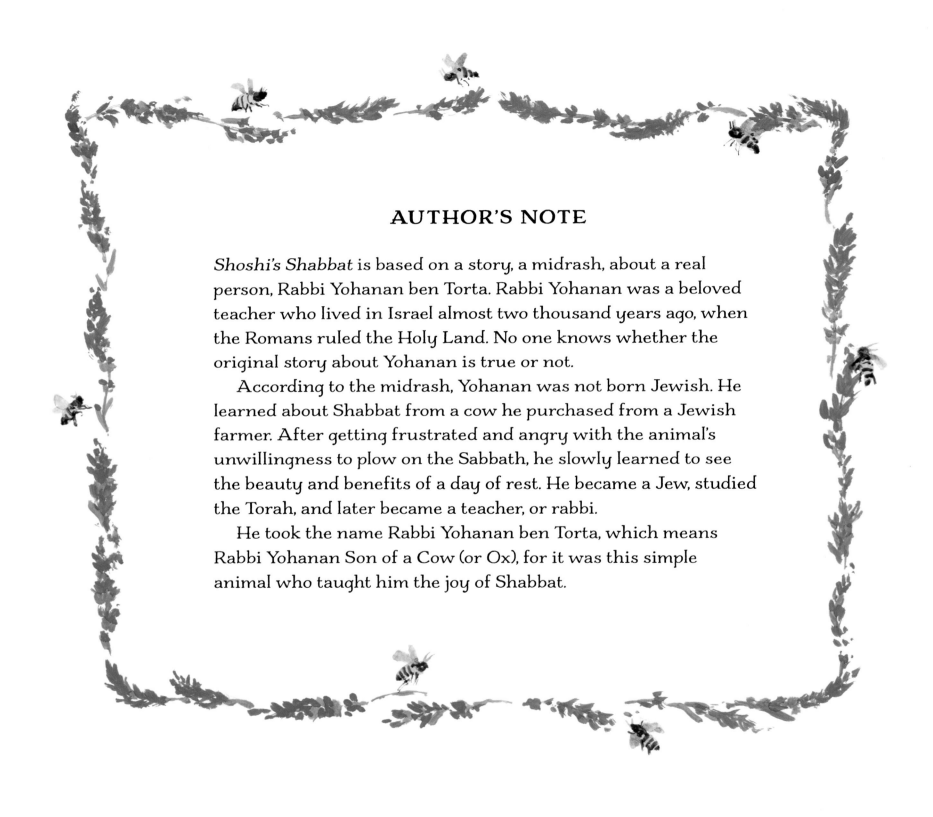

AUTHOR'S NOTE

Shoshi's Shabbat is based on a story, a midrash, about a real person, Rabbi Yohanan ben Torta. Rabbi Yohanan was a beloved teacher who lived in Israel almost two thousand years ago, when the Romans ruled the Holy Land. No one knows whether the original story about Yohanan is true or not.

According to the midrash, Yohanan was not born Jewish. He learned about Shabbat from a cow he purchased from a Jewish farmer. After getting frustrated and angry with the animal's unwillingness to plow on the Sabbath, he slowly learned to see the beauty and benefits of a day of rest. He became a Jew, studied the Torah, and later became a teacher, or rabbi.

He took the name Rabbi Yohanan ben Torta, which means Rabbi Yohanan Son of a Cow (or Ox), for it was this simple animal who taught him the joy of Shabbat.

The Hebrew Bible teaches that animals as well as people should have a day of rest. I was drawn to this ancient tale for two reasons: my love and respect for animals and my love of Shabbat.

In the midrash, the "plowing heifer" has no name. The name Shoshi came to me one Shabbat afternoon as I was watching bees buzzing around the lavender and roses in my garden. As I contemplated her sweet yet determined personality, I knew this little ox would be the perfect creature to teach Yohanan the mitzvah, the commandment or good deed, of keeping Shabbat.

My love for Shabbat has grown over the years. I believe that today, more than ever, it is a precious gift to all of us. To slow down one day a week, to be in nature or with friends and family, to enjoy a meal with others without rushing to yet another activity, and to feel gratitude is to experience its sweetness.

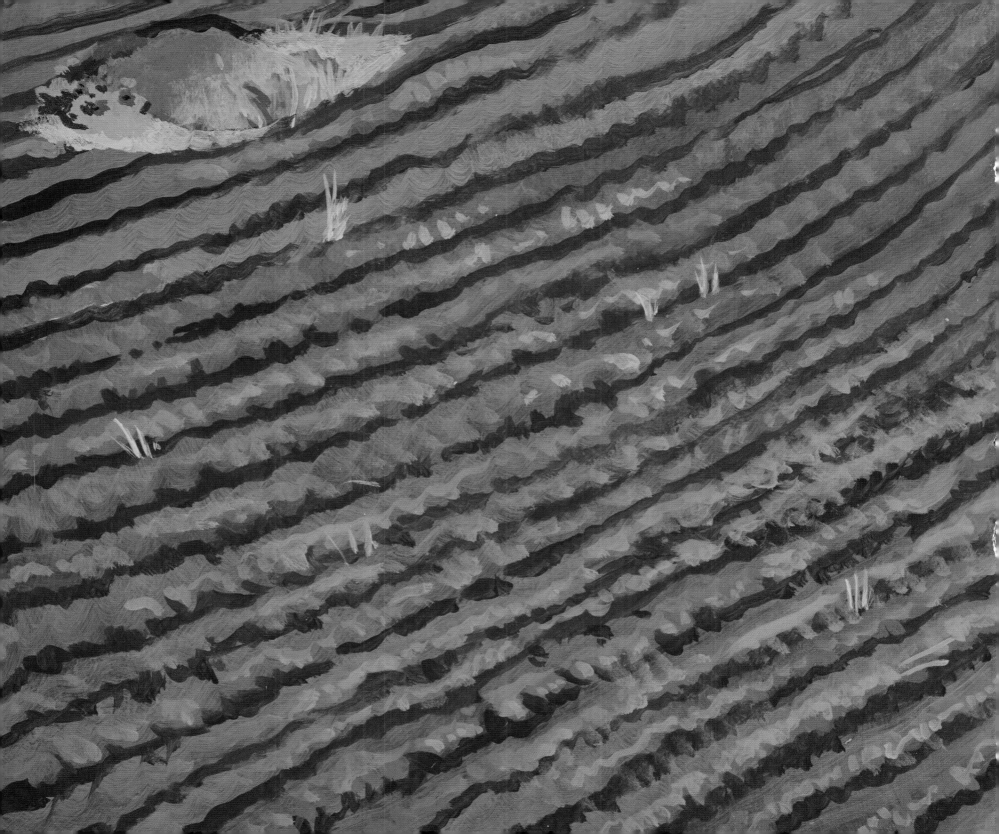